# Truck Stuck

Sallie Wolf

Illustrated by
Andy Robert Davies

ini Charlesbridge

To my parents, Rosamond and
Barton Myers Lloyd—S. W.

To my family, thank you for your support—A. R. D.

2009 First paperback edition
Text copyright © 2008 by Sallie Wolf
Illustrations copyright © 2008 by Andy Robert Davies
All rights reserved, including the right of reproduction in whole
or in part in any form. Charlesbridge and colophon are
registered trademarks of Charlesbridge Publishing, Inc.

Published by Charlesbridge
85 Main Street
Watertown, MA 02472
(617) 926-0329
www.charlesbridge.com

**Library of Congress Cataloging-in-Publication Data**
Wolf, Sallie.
    Truck stuck / Sallie Wolf ; illustrated by Andy Robert Davies.
        p. cm.
    Summary: Illustrations and simple rhyming text tell the story
of a big truck that gets stuck under a bridge.
        ISBN 978-1-58089-119-6 (reinforced for library use)
        ISBN 978-1-58089-257-5 (softcover)
        ISBN 978-1-60734-015-7 (ebook)
    [1. Trucks—Fiction.  2. Vehicles—Fiction.  3. Stories in rhyme.]
    I. Davies, Andy Robert, ill.  II. Title.
    PZ8.3.W8425Tr 2008
    [E]—dc22            2007002282

Printed in China
(hc) 10 9 8 7 6 5 4 3 2
(sc) 10 9 8 7 6 5 4 3 2

Illustrations done in pen and ink and manipulated digitally
Display type and text type set in Billy, designed by
    Dave Buck of SparkyType, New Zealand
Color separations by Chroma Graphics, Singapore
Manufactured by Regent Publishing Services, Hong Kong
Printed December 2013 in Shenzhen, Guangdong, China
Production supervision by Brian G. Walker
Designed by Susan Mallory Sherman

Big truck.

Viaduct.
Uh-oh. Too low.
Stop, truck!

Truck stuck.

Beep Beep!!!

limousine, exterminator.

All stuck. Move that truck!

Street sweeper,    tree chipper,

delivery van,     produce man.

Let us pass. Step on the gas!

Traffic cops.
Whistles blow.

Phones to fix. Concrete to mix.

BEEP!

Lawns to mow.          Scouts on the go.

TV crew pushing through.

BIG tow truck,
yellow and green,
on the scene.
Let us through!

No need to shout—
let the air out!

All clear.
Big cheer!
Out of here.

Good luck,
big truck.

Back up, truck.
Unstuck.